Tania's Palace

PRAISE FOR *STORYSHARES*

"One of the brightest innovators and game-changers in the education industry."
– Forbes

"Your success in applying research-validated practices to promote literacy serves as a valuable model for other organizations seeking to create evidence-based literacy programs."
- Library of Congress

"We need powerful social and educational innovation, and Storyshares is breaking new ground. The organization addresses critical problems facing our students and teachers. I am excited about the strategies it brings to the collective work of making sure every student has an equal chance in life."
– Teach For America

"Around the world, this is one of the up-and-coming trailblazers changing the landscape of literacy and education."
- International Literacy Association

"It's the perfect idea. There's really nothing like this. I mean wow, this will be a wonderful experience for young people."   - Andrea Davis Pinkney, Executive Director, Scholastic

"Reading for meaning opens opportunities for a lifetime of learning. Providing emerging readers with engaging texts that are designed to offer both challenges and support for each individual will improve their lives for years to come. Storyshares is a wonderful start."
- David Rose, Co-founder of CAST & UDL

Tania's Palace

Brian Kirchner

STORYSHARES

Story Share, Inc.
New York. Boston. Philadelphia

Copyright © 2022 by Brian Kirchner

All rights reserved.

Published in the United States by Story Share, Inc.

The characters and events in this book are fictitious. Any similarity to real persons, living or dead, is entirely coincidental.

Storyshares
Story Share, Inc.
24 N. Bryn Mawr Avenue #340
Bryn Mawr, PA 19010-3304
www.storyshares.org

Inspiring reading with a new kind of book.

Interest Level: High School
Grade Level Equivalent: 4.0

9781642611168

Book design by Storyshares

Printed in the United States of America

Storyshares Presents

1

So, here's how it all went down...

One Thursday evening in early spring, the year after the whole mess with Derek Bodley and the spray paint, my buddy X and I were throwing down some jams in my garage. We were sounding good, working through a new arrangement of some B.B. King blues tunes that our band, the People Movers, was going to play at our very first live gig.

The gig was a dance at Redford Union High School, where we were all sophomores, and it was coming up fast. That Saturday, in fact, April 22nd, only two days away. The band consisted of X (whose real name was Xavier Maplethorpe) on vocals, me on lead guitar, Kenji Omura on bass, and Yusuf Karout on drums.

Kenji and Yusuf were due to show up soon. It was warm, really warm for April in southeast Michigan, and the trees were just starting to leaf out and the sun was shining. All in all, a good day to practice.

Yeah, things were looking good and feeling even better that Thursday night.

Until...

Who comes sauntering down the sidewalk but Derek Bodley himself, in the flesh, skinny as ever, strolling along with his narrow face staring down at the concrete. He had on scuffed blue jeans and a KISS T-shirt so faded you could barely make out the band's logo. On his head was his trademark red baseball cap with the tired old political slogan on it. The cap, once bright crimson, was now stained and faded.

Come to think of it, that cap was a perfect symbol for what was left of the political career of the man who'd gotten elected by that stupid, empty slogan. He was now under all kinds of indictments, investigations, the works.

He spent most of his time tweeting from his bedroom in the White House while his aides actually ran things, sort of. I'd heard that he hadn't come out of the bedroom in three months. Some people said it was six.

Bodley had a cigarette hanging out of one corner of his mouth, smoke drifting up in a gray coil. I could see him blinking as the smoke got in his eyes.

I didn't know when he'd started smoking, but it really didn't do anything to improve his image. He probably thought it made him look tough, but he just looked like a skinny dude trying to look cool. Personally, I think looking cool is overrated. People are at their best when they're just being themselves and not trying to impress anyone. Just my two cents.

Bodley stopped at the end of my driveway. He stared at us; at least, he turned his skinny face in our general direction. He actually seemed to be staring at a point in space above us and to the left. Bodley never looked you right in the eye. He was always sidling, looking this way and that like he was searching for an escape route or something.

X stopped wailing out his version of "How Blue Can You Get," and I stopped just before hitting a power E chord on my Fender Strat. The music echoed off the houses across the street and died out, leaving nothing but the birds twittering to break the silence.

Finally, X spoke up. "What do you want, Bodley?"

Bodley didn't say anything, but he took the cigarette from his mouth and held it between his fingers. He pointed at X with the cigarette.

"You. Yeah, you. Skinny chump with the big, dumb hair. You thought you got me, didn't you? Last summer. Yeah, thought you were so clever, right? You ain't clever. You ain't smart."

His cigarette jittered in his hand, puffing off smoke like a chimney as he continued pointing at X.

"You know what my dad did when the cops told him what happened? Huh? You wanna know what he did to me? He put me in the hospital, that's what! Yeah, the hospital! Two broken ribs, two black eyes, and a broken arm. When he got done beating on me, he sent me to live with his brother in Florida for eight months. I was there all winter. Just got back last week. Never thought I'd be glad to back in this dump of a city."

"Well, Florida for the winter doesn't sound so bad," I said.

"The hell it doesn't! My uncle's a drunk. Lives in the black mangrove swamps near Saint Pete. Hellhole full of mosquitoes. My dad sent me there as an extra punishment. And you wanna know what my uncle did? Look at this!"

Bodley lifted his T-shirt up high enough to expose most of the left side of his ribcage. It was covered with about a dozen whitish, circular scars.

"Wanna know what these are? Cigarette burns, you scumbags. Courtesy of Uncle Ronnie."

X and I stared in shock at the old wounds on Bodley's pale skin. Neither of us had any love for the guy, but we sure didn't like thinking about his dad, Vince Bodley, and his uncle abusing him because of what went down last summer. But Vince Bodley was the kind of man who would do it. He was meaner than a rabid dog. And it didn't surprise me one bit to learn that Vince's brother wasn't any better.

"This is your fault, Maplethorpe," said Bodley, pointing at his side. "You might as well have done it yourself."

X shook his head, making his huge Afro sway back and forth like tall grass in a windy field. "Look, bro, for real, me and Carlos are sorry your pops and your uncle did you like this. But it ain't on us, man. Can you dig that? We had to do the right thing."

"Yeah, X isn't lying," I chimed in. "You trying to frame our man Yusuf like that? That was most uncool, Derek."

"I ain't talkin' to you, you beaner," Bodley snarled, glaring at me.

I put my hands up as if to say, Sure, man, whatever you say.

"Hey, it's the man himself!" said X, a big grin breaking out on his face.

Coming down the street on a brand-new Schwinn ten-speed was our drummer.

Let me explain a little bit about Yusuf. First of all, he's the most butt-kicking drummer you ever heard. I mean, he could give Neil Peart from Rush a run for his money. (Okay, that's a bit of an exaggeration. But not by much.)

Last summer, our band put out an ad looking for a drummer, and Yusuf was the first person to respond. We learned that, aside from being a great skins man and all-around good dude, he and his family were refugees from Syria who'd settled in our town of Redford, Michigan, just west of Detroit. It was just Yusuf and his folks (who are also *trés* cool, by the way), but he'd had a little sister who died trying to get out of their home country.

Pretty soon after he joined our band, everyone's favorite knucklehead, Derek Bodley, tried to frame Yusuf for some nasty graffiti spray-painted on the Bodley garage. The rest of the band did some investigating and found proof of Bodley doing the deed himself.

Thus, the cigarette burns and everything else his dad inflicted on him. And I was dead serious when I said I was sorry about what Derek's dad did to him. I know X was, too.

Anyway, there was our skins man, pedaling his new bike, dressed in one of his usual crazy outfits. This time he had on really tight black leather pants, a bright orange

Abercrombie and Fitch polo shirt, knee-length white socks that looked like they'd be at home on some NBA player, and huge neon-yellow running shoes. And, of course, he had his trademark straw cowboy hat with the American flag bandanna wrapped around it perched on his head.

There was a girl with him, riding her own bike. Tall, with dark, curly hair, skin that was a shade or two darker than Yusuf's own mocha tones, and a big smile. She and Yusuf were racing, and she was winning. Not too surprising, considering Yusuf's only about five-foot-three and this girl probably had at least four inches on him.

They screeched to a stop in my driveway, both of them panting and smiling. The way they were looking at each other told me there was something more than just biking going on with them. The girl held her phone up to take a quick selfie with Yusuf. They both grinned into the camera and then at each other.

"Hey, you guys!" said Yusuf, setting his bike down on the driveway. He barely glanced at Bodley, who was busy giving the girl the hairy eyeball. "This is Tania. Tania Yates. She lives in my building."

"Hey, how you doin', Tania?" said X.

"What's up?" I said.

"Hi," she said. "So this is your band?"

"Yeah," said Yusuf. "We're awesome. Just wait." To X and me he said, "Where's Kenji?"

"He's on his way," said X. "He'll be here in a few."

Yusuf and Tania came into the garage, and Tania set her phone down carefully on a stack of old milk crates that served as shelves for some of my dad's tools.

Bodley was still outside on the driveway, and he was really glowering at Tania now. I didn't like it. Nobody else seemed to have noticed. They had all forgotten about Derek.

"Let me show you some beats!" said Yusuf to Tania, taking a seat on the stool behind his old Ludwig kit and picking up his sticks. (He'd painted them a funny shade of orange, called Cactus Crimson, last summer. That paint figured into the whole Bodley drama, but that's another story.)

Tania moved to join him. She took a seat on the old leather sofa next to his kit.

2

Just then, Derek stepped into the garage. Actually, he sidled in, like he always did. He never walked straight, just like he never looked straight at you. Yeah, he sidled on in, past the milk crates and my dad's workbench, past X and his microphone, and up to Yusuf's kit.

"Man, go on outta here, jet!" said X.

"Yeah, Bodley, what he said," I told him. "We have a practice to do."

Bodley put a pained expression on his long, narrow face. "You guys, I just want to hear you play!" he said, raising his hands in an "I'm innocent" gesture. "I like your music, for real." He snorted phlegm. "It's good! Come on, Yusuf, play me some drums, bro."

Yusuf stared at him. "I'm not your bro, Bodley. Why don't you leave now, like X and Carlos asked you to?"

As always, Yusuf's tone was calm and polite. I don't think the dude could get mad if he tried. I guess that's what happens when your sister gets killed and your family goes through hell. It puts life's problems in perspective.

Bodley looked even more aggrieved. He now looked like the world's tallest four-year-old who wasn't getting a lollipop. He sat down defiantly on the leather sofa next to Tania, who promptly got up and stepped away from him.

We all looked at each other. X shrugged. "I dunno, fellas, guess he ain't hurting anything," he said. "Way I see it, though, it's your call, Carlos, seeing as it's your garage and all." X nodded at his own words as if they were the sagest advice he'd ever heard.

"I guess it's okay by me," I said, thinking about Derek's cigarette burns and feeling some sympathy for the guy.

Looking back on it later, I realized all the trouble that went down over the next few days could have been avoided if I'd remembered one simple rule: the Derek Bodleys of the world will take advantage of your sympathy and use it against you. I've never believed there are very many people like him, but when you run across one, you need to watch out. They bite.

"That's cool," said Derek. "And you know what? Just to be nice, I'll get off the couch so your girlfriend can sit here. Pretty obvious she doesn't like me."

He got up off the sofa and sidled over to the milk crates and leaned against them. He crossed his arms and surveyed the rest of us expectantly.

Tania sat back down on the cracked brown leather. She nodded at Derek but looked cautious. "Thanks, man."

Bodley tipped her a wink. I rolled my eyes. What a piece of work.

"Right on!" said X. "And look who's boogying up the driveway as we speak!"

It was Kenji, wearing one of his signature Hawaiian shirts and carrying the big, black case that contained his Fender Jazz bass.

"Hey, you guys!" said Kenji with a grin. "What's up? You ready to—" He stopped in mid-sentence when he registered Derek Bodley's presence. Kenji looked confused.

"What's he doing here?" Kenji asked me, but Derek answered.

"Just hanging with you guys, waiting for the jams to start," he said.

Kenji gave him a weird look.

"It's cool, bro," said X. "Carlos and Yusuf already gave it the OK. It's all good, baby."

Kenji didn't look convinced, but he said nothing. He started unpacking his guitar.

"When you guys gonna start playing?" said Bodley in a nasally whine. He slouched against the stack of milk crates, making them wobble a bit.

"Hey, Bodley, watch it!" I said, pointing behind him. "Don't knock that stuff over, man."

Bodley glowered at me but straightened up, taking his weight off the stack. "That better?"

I just nodded and started tuning up my guitar, an old Fender Stratocaster my dad had given me when I turned ten years old. I'd been playing it ever since.

"Hey, you got some new stuff on that axe?" said X, pointing at the body of my Fender. "Looks like it."

I nodded. "Yeah, I finally got the ones for Zimbabwe and Uruguay."

For the last two months I'd been collecting decals of country flags and sticking them on the guitar. At this point, they covered almost every square inch of it, front and back. I had almost every country in the world, now that I'd gotten Zimbabwe and Uruguay from eBay.

I pointed to the milk crates behind Derek. "Got a few more over there I haven't put on yet."

Kenji squinted through his glasses. "I don't see 'em," he said.

I checked it out, and saw that Kenji was right —
they weren't where I'd left them. I'd put them on top of a
pile of old *Popular Mechanics* magazines on the second
shelf, and there was nothing there now. A quick scan of
the floor told me they hadn't fallen off, either.

"I just put those things there this morning!" I said,
looking at my bandmates. "Hey, X, didn't you see them
there when you got here?"

"Right on, my brother," he replied. "For sure."

"Then what—"

I stopped and turned to stare at Bodley. He was
still smirking at me, and slowly backing out of the garage.
He raised his hands to show they were empty.

"What?" he said. "What?" He tried to sound
innocent, but the irritating grin on his face told another
story.

"Bodley, you moron!" I said, taking off my guitar
and leaning it against a wall. "You grabbed them, didn't
you?" I stepped toward him. X and Kenji did the same.
Yusuf and Tania watched from the back of the garage.

"You idiots are blinder than..." He trailed off, struggling for a metaphor. "...than a blind guy!" he finished.

"Say what, fool?" said X, laughing. "Man, Carlos has you dead right. You swiped those decals. You know it, I know it, Carlos knows it, and soon everybody here is gonna know it."

Bodley's sneering grin faltered for a moment, probably because X sounded so confident. And if X sounded confident about something, he was nearly always right about it. In fact, I couldn't remember him ever being wrong about anything once he'd thought it through.

Here's the deal on X: His full name was Xavier Montgomery Maplethorpe, and he was a genius. That's not an exaggeration, either. He'd somehow gotten Sherlock Holmes's brain transplanted under his giant Afro. The dude could figure things out like a boss! And now he had that tone in his voice that told me he knew Bodley had my flag stickers, and that's all I needed to hear.

Now, X was standing right in front of Derek with his long, brown arms crossed, smiling down at the shorter kid from his six-foot altitude. Bodley looked sidelong at X, his head turned to one side.

"Come on, hand them over," I said. "We know you got 'em."

Bodley stood for a moment, just staring off over X's shoulder somewhere, maybe trying to decide whether my decals were worth the trouble. Finally he shrugged and dug into the right back pocket of his beat-up, greasy jeans.

"Whatever, here," he snorted, dropping a handful of slim clear plastic envelopes on the ground. I recognized the flags of Liechtenstein, Mongolia, and Palau on three of them. There were two more that landed face down, but I knew they were Grenada and Lesotho. "Happy now? Stickers are for little kids, anyway, you losers."

I bent down and picked them up. "Guess you aren't staying for practice after all, huh?" I said. "I'm heartbroken."

Bodley laughed. "Hell, no. You guys suck royally. I'm gone." And he was.

3

"Hey, where's my phone?"

This came from Tania, who was standing in front of the stack of milk crates, hands on hips, staring down at the spot where she'd put her cell phone when she and Yusuf had arrived.

Practice was over, and we were packing up our gear. X was practicing a few James Brown moves he'd learned on YouTube — he wanted to show them off at our gig. He stopped mid-gyration and looked over at Tania.

"Aw, you ain't saying—"

"It's gone, yeah," finished Tania. "I set it down right here before you guys started."

"That's where Derek was standing," said Yusuf, getting out from behind his kit and coming over to Tania.

She nodded. "He creeps me out. He's the one who almost got your family deported last year? He looks like Wormtongue in *Lord of the Rings*."

"He's the one," said Yusuf. "I think he stole your phone somehow."

"How could he have taken it?" she said. "We were all right here the whole time. He a magician or something?"

"No," said Yusuf. "But he's... devious. Is that the word? Yeah, devious." Yusuf had been in the States for over a year now, and his English was really good, but he occasionally still had some trouble finding just the right word.

"It was the decals, peeps," said X. "When he threw Carlos's decals all over the ground. It was a distraction. That's when he swiped the phone." He looked angry. "I shoulda noticed that before he took off."

We all knew X was right. Bodley must have grabbed Tania's phone while everyone else was watching me pick up my decals. Yusuf was right. *Devious.*

"Your phone have a passcode?" I asked.

"Yes," Tania said.

"So your stuff's safe, at least. I don't think Bodley's exactly hacker material. He'll never get into it."

Tania didn't look very comforted. "I guess so," she said. "Does he live around here?"

"Sadly, yes," said Kenji, zipping his bass into its black gig bag and hefting the bag onto one shoulder.

"Just a few blocks from here. He goes to our school, too."

"Yusuf, can I use your phone?" asked Tania. "I'm going to call the police."

"No problem," he replied, grinning from ear to ear and pulling his cell from his back pocket. He handed it over. He continued smiling at Tania after she took the phone.

"What're you grinning at, man?" Tania asked, smiling a little herself in spite of how upset she was. "Stop it, you're gonna make me blush."

"Hold up, sister," said X. Tania looked at him questioningly. "The Redford P.D. probably can't jump right on this. They ain't got enough cops to go around, and most of 'em are usually working bigger stuff. Could be a while before they get your phone back."

Tania frowned. Her skin, normally a shade or two darker than X's own, flushed an even deeper coffee color, and her dark brown eyes flashed with anger.

"Then what do you suggest, X?" she said, her voice tight. "I'd love to hear whatever it is you have in mind."

X, unperturbed by Tania's sarcasm, said, "Already got it figured out. Gotta jet and talk to my pops to get things rolling." X's dad, Monty Maplethorpe, was a semi-retired Redford police detective who helped us out once in a while. "Promise me you won't make that call until you hear back from me. Can you dig it?"

Without waiting for an answer, X took off, loping away down the street toward his house on his stork-like legs. Kenji left a minute later. Tania and Yusuf and I stood in the garage, staring at the spot where her cell phone had been. She was still upset.

"X better know what he's doing," she said. "I need my phone back. I don't need it hacked into or sold online or something." She shook her head, and her brown curls bounced.

"You can trust X," I said. "Remember, he's the one who saved Yusuf and his family."

Tania's Palace

4

A half-hour later, Tania, Yusuf, and I were still hanging in the garage, Yusuf practicing some tricky rhythms and Tania and I just chatting (loudly, so we could hear each other over Yusuf's banging). Turned out she was a ham radio aficionado. She had her own set, and she and her mom had built an antenna on the roof of the apartment building they shared with the Karouts. She told me she'd talked to people from as far away as Alaska.

I have to be honest: I'd never have guessed she was the amateur radio type. She looked more like a champion pole-vaulter or something, lean and muscular and athletic. And that wasn't too far off, actually. When I asked her if she played any sports, she rattled off a bunch. Basketball, tennis, cross-country, and a few others. Pretty impressive. National Honor Society, too.

Most of all, I learned that besides being a radio geek and an athlete, Tania Yates was just cool, down-to-earth, and easy to talk to. Smart, athletic, good-looking, and cool. I could understand why Yusuf liked her.

At one point, I looked over at my buddy as he worked his kit, his big straw cowboy hat wobbling around but somehow staying on his head. I was happy for the guy. I'd seen the way he'd looked at Tania all through practice. He was really into this girl. And I think she was into him, too.

"I can't wait to introduce Yusuf to my mom," Tania said. "She'll love him. Plus, she always wants to know about other countries. Always reading books about China, Russia, the Middle East, whatever. I don't know how she finds the time. She's been raising my two brothers and me ever since my dad took off on us five years ago. But that was fine with me. He was a jerk. We're better off without him. Sorry, am I sharing too much?" She looked at me, frowning. "Sometimes I just get talking and it just sorta comes out."

"Nope, it's all good," I said. "It's good info, actually, seeing as how I have final approval over all of my man Yusuf's girlfriends."

At this, Tania flushed and covered her mouth, trying to stifle a giggle. After a moment she got it under control. "I'm not his girlfriend, Carlos, what're you talking about, man? We're buddies, he's cool. That's all."

I nodded. "Okay. Sure."

The fact that I wasn't the slightest bit convinced must have been written all over my face, because she waved her hand dismissively.

"Okay, mister rock star, you think whatever you want to," she said, but she couldn't hide a smile.

Just then, X returned, bounding into the garage, Afro waving around like a cloud on a windy day.

"What's happenin', brothers and sisters?" he said. "Yo, Tania, my pops got us hooked up. Check this: he called in a favor with an old buddy of his on the Redford

P.D. Guy named Sergeant Reese. This guy's gonna, uh, motivate that knucklehead Bodley to turn in your phone at the station."

"'Motivate?'" I said. "What's that mean, dude? They gonna pick Bodley up and throw him in jail overnight or something?"

"Yeah, X, what's up with that?" said Tania. "I want my phone back from Derek, but I don't want anything bad to happen to him." She paused, thinking. "Nothing really bad, anyway."

"No worries," said X. "Nothin' like that. No arresting, no third-degree questions under a hot light bulb, none of that noir stuff. What's gonna happen is, Sergeant Reese is gonna put out a bulletin. Kinda like a wanted poster. It'll have a description of the phone, when and where it was taken, and best of all, in big letters, it'll say there's a reward of one hundred dollars for returning it. It'll be posted all over the neighborhood and Redford High, too. Bodley'll be sure to see it."

"One hundred dollars?" said Yusuf, putting down his sticks and getting up from behind the drum kit. "Who's going to pay a hundred dollars?"

"Not me," said Tania. "I don't have that kind of cash."

X shook his head. "Check it out: the reward ain't gonna be in cash. It's gonna be a — wait for it — a Barnes and Noble gift card!" He started laughing, his lean frame doubling over like a gantry collapsing in on itself. "Gift card! Can you dig it, my friends?"

"Wait," I said. "Chill out, X. Explain. So if Bodley returns the phone, the cops are gonna give him a bookstore gift card? Why? And who's going to pay for it?"

"My pops has one from last Christmas he doesn't want. He hates Barnes and Noble for some reason. He was always a Borders guy. He got righteously torqued when Borders went under. Now he won't set foot inside B and N. Won't go on their website either. He says he blames them for Borders tanking."

He suddenly realized we were all giving him odd looks. "Yeah, yeah, I know, it's weird. What're you gonna do? People are funky." He shrugged. "Anyway, that's where the gift card's comin' from. You imagine Bodley's face when they hand it to him? He's gonna have a stroke!" He started chuckling again.

"It's brilliant," said Yusuf. He was laughing, too. "The bulletin won't say anything about the money being in cash, right?"

"Right on."

Tania nodded, smiling. "Thanks, X. And thank your pops for me, too, okay?"

"For sure, sister."

We were all feeling pretty good right then, at the thought of Tania getting her phone back and Derek Bodley getting handed a piece of plastic instead of a wad of cash.

It wouldn't last long.

5

The wild applause, whistles, and cheering swelled in the Redford Union High School gym as the last notes of the Rolling Stones's "Satisfaction" echoed from the cinderblock walls and faded. We all stood up on the small stage, taking it all in. There were probably more than two hundred people packed into the place, and they were all yelling for us.

The gig had gone better than any of us had hoped. We'd played a full set plus two encores, all four of us right in sync with each other, the music flowing perfectly. Everyone in the crowd was smiling.

I caught sight of Yusuf, standing behind his kit with his straw cowboy hat on, staring at someone in the front row, right up against the stage. It was Tania, of course. She was beaming and clapping and whistling, and giving Yusuf thumbs-up signs. It made me happy for the guy. He deserved this, after everything he'd been through.

The only blemish on the night's festivities came about halfway through our set. I happened to look over the crowd to the back of the gym, and I saw someone back there with a red baseball cap on, leaning against the wall next to one of the doors. It was hard to tell for sure whether it was Derek Bodley, since there were spotlights shining in my face, but when I looked again a few minutes later, whoever it had been was gone.

Finally, the noise died down and the crowd began to filter out of the gym in small groups. Their chatter echoed in the big room. Then that was gone, too, and we began packing up our equipment. The school's AV technician, Rudy Murphy, appeared from backstage to help out.

"You guys rocked it to the rafters tonight!" he exclaimed. "Unbelievable! You had this place wrapped around your fingers." He winked at Yusuf. "And I saw that chick you were eyeballin', my friend." Rudy waggled his eyebrows up and down. "When I was your age, I woulda been after her like a dog chasin' a squirrel."

Yusuf stared back at Rudy, smiling a little but clearly puzzled. Rudy was originally from Texas and had the accent to prove it. It was thicker than barbeque sauce. He was an aging hippie who still wore his gray hair long, usually in a ponytail, and loved to talk about all the Grateful Dead shows he'd been to back in the day. And though he never mentioned it to us, we all knew he'd consumed a lot more than just beer and potato chips in his time.

X spoke up. "What my southern brother is sayin', Yusuf, is that he approves of your girlfriend."

Yusuf shook his head, his face going two shades darker than it already was. "She's not my girlfriend, you guys! Really. We're just buddies."

Kenji, X, and I all looked at each other. Kenji was the first to start laughing. Then X and I joined in. Even Rudy started chuckling as he coiled up amplifier cables.

I clapped Yusuf on the back, making his big old hat wobble dangerously. "Dude, if you say so. If you say so."

Just then, the subject of the conversation appeared at the front of the stage. She was still flushed and sweaty from dancing nonstop for over an hour.

"You guys blew the freaking house down!" she said as she clambered up onto the stage and ran over to us. Her dark, curly hair was done up in cornrows tonight, and she wore a simple blue jersey top and black jeans. "What a show! When're you playing again? I want to put it in my phone." She whipped her cell out of her back pocket.

The fake bulletin had worked. Bodley had turned the phone in to the cops less than twenty-four hours after the bulletin had been put up. According to X's dad, who heard it from his Redford P.D. buddies, Derek had thrown a monster tantrum when they'd handed him his gift card: yelling, swearing, even threatening to sue. The whole works. He'd ended up getting escorted out of the station by two officers. And Tania had her phone back.

"We don't know when the next gig will be," said Kenji.

"You all kiddin' me?" said Rudy. It came out like "Yawl keedin me?" "The way you played tonight, the school will be kissing your feet to play the next dance. You know what that is, right?"

"Prom," I said.

Rudy nodded. "You got it, man. Prom. Bet you anything Mr. LeBlanc gets in touch by the end of the week about having you guys play. Prom's only a month away."

Burt LeBlanc was Redford High's principal, a guy built like a linebacker who wore suits ten years out of style. But he was popular with the students because he took a personal interest in everyone at the school. He was always on the hallways, talking to people and exchanging fist bumps and high fives.

With most principals, this kind of thing would have made them the butt of a hundred different jokes behind his back, but not Mr. LeBlanc. He was relatable, if you know what I mean. He was real. You got the feeling he wasn't putting on an act.

"When's prom?" asked Tania.

"May 26th," I said. "Like Rudy said, only a month away."

"Thanks, Carlos," she said, and tapped at her phone for a minute. "Got it on my calendar." She slipped the phone back into her pocket. "I gotta run. Supposed to meet up with my mom for dinner. People Movers rock!"

With that, she jumped down off the stage and strode toward one of the gym doors, her long brown arms swinging, her fingers snapping. We could hear her singing one of the tunes we'd played that night.

I glanced at Yusuf. He was staring after her with his mouth slightly open.

"Dude," I said. "Pick your jaw up off the floor before bugs crawl down your throat."

Everyone laughed. A door banged closed as Tania left the gym.

The next time I saw her, she'd barely be conscious and I'd be trying to pull her out of a very tight spot.

6

"You guys, Tania never came home last night!"

This came from Yusuf as he burst into my garage, where the rest of us were setting up for practice. It was Sunday, the morning after the gig, and X, Kenji, and I were hanging in the garage, still juked on the vibe from Saturday night.

Until now, at least.

I knew our drummer was truly freaked because he'd forgotten to put on his straw cowboy hat. It was one of the few times I'd seen him without it. His dark hair stuck up in all directions like he'd just rolled out of bed. Or like he'd been running his hands through it a lot.

"Whoa, bro, jump back," said X, holding his hands up, palms toward Yusuf. The shorter kid practically skidded to a stop in the middle of the garage next to X's mic stand, panting and sweating. "Chill for a sec. Take some breaths. Find your Zen place, baby."

Yusuf looked puzzled at the Zen reference, and I made a mental note to explain later. He paced around in a circle.

"How can I calm down?" he said, his Syrian accent thicker than usual because he was so upset. "Tania is gone. She never came home after the gig! Her mom talked to my mom, she wanted to know if I'd seen her. I haven't seen her since the gig. She hasn't called or texted me, either. And she hasn't answered any of mine. I was starting to get a little worried about her, and then her mom called me. They were supposed to meet for dinner last night and Tania never showed up."

"Where were they gonna meet?" asked X. I could tell his mental gears were already turning.

"Hamburger Palace on Grand River Avenue," said Yusuf, still pacing.

I grabbed his shoulders and guided him toward the old leather sofa next to his drum kit.

He stood for a second, like he wasn't sure where he was, then let out a long *whoosh* of breath and collapsed into the sofa's deep cushions. "She was going to tell her mom about our gig."

"She didn't say anything to you about going anywhere else before she met up with her mom?" asked X.

Yusuf shook his head. "No. Nothing. She told me she was going straight to the restaurant."

"Maybe she just met up with friends instead and forgot to tell her mom," offered Kenji. I knew he was trying to help Yusuf feel better, but it fell flat. We all knew she wouldn't have been gone for three whole days.

"Tania's mom call the cops?" asked X.

"Yes, of course she did, X! They told her they can't put out the Amber Alert unless they know she's been kidnapped. Tania's mom thinks her dad grabbed her. Her dad's a... a bum. She called him a bum. She said he's been fighting her for custody for two years. But the police said they can't issue the alert unless they know Tania didn't just spend the night somewhere else."

"Maybe that's what happened," offered Kenji.

Yusuf shook his head rapidly. "No. No. Tania wouldn't do that, stay overnight somewhere without telling her mom. Her mom said she told the police all of this, but they said they can't do anything yet. X, is that right, man? Can't the police do anything? Can't they send out the Amber Alert or something?" Yusuf was beginning to sound frantic again.

X dropped himself onto the sofa next to Yusuf and put a long arm around Yusuf's shoulders. "Bro, she's right on about the Amber Alert. My pops told me once they can't put those out if they think there's a possibility the missing kid just got P.O.d at her folks and decided to have a sleepover somewhere."

"But—" Yusuf began to protest.

X gave Yusuf's shoulders a squeeze. "I said they can't do it if they think there's a possibility," he said. "But they don't know Tania like you do. You know, and we all know, she didn't just skip out on her mom. Like you said, she wouldn't do that."

Yusuf nodded. He looked close to tears. I really felt for him. He'd lost a little sister when his family escaped from Syria, and now the girl he was totally gaga over might be missing. I could understand where he was coming from.

"Hey, X," I said. "Maybe your dad can give us some inside 411 on this. Maybe tell us if there's something we can be doing now. Beats sitting here worrying, am I right?"

X snapped his fingers. "You read my mind, Carlos. Let's bounce."

7

"Best thing you boys can do is stay outta the way."

Montgomery Maplethorpe made this pronouncement from his usual throne: an ancient overstuffed armchair made of cracked red leather that groaned under the man's weight. Detective Maplethorpe probably ran close to three hundred pounds. His bad leg, the result of being shot while on the job with the Redford P.D., rested on an equally ancient ottoman that matched the chair.

His signature cigar was plugged into one corner of his mouth, giving off billows of foul smoke. I tried not to breathe as I stood there with my bandmates in the Maplethorpe living room, surrounded by framed commendations and photos of X's dad with various bigwigs.

"I know Winnie Yates," the detective continued. "She's good people, but she's private. She don't want you fellas nosing around in this business about her daughter. Just leave it to the law, boys."

"But the cops ain't doing anything, pops!" said X. "They can't put out the Amber Alert yet. They can't declare her officially missing, either. So we just supposed to wait until Tania turns up—" He cut himself off, glancing at Yusuf with a chagrined look. Yusuf's mocha-colored skin turned a shade or two paler. "Sorry, bro. You know that ain't gonna happen. She's gonna turn up."

"That's right, Xavier," said Detective Maplethorpe. "Ninety percent of these cases where a teenager disappears, the kid turns up just fine a day or two later when they're done bein' mad over whatever they're mad about that week. Might even be ninety-five percent. I forget."

"What about the ten percent?" said Yusuf. "What about those cases?"

Detective Maplethorpe shook his head, making the stream of smoke from his stogie waver like an uneasy ghost. "There ain't no need to talk about that, Yusuf. Now, I know you're worried. I understand. But listen to an old soldier who's been down this particular road more times than he cares to remember: the missing kid turns up fine most every time."

We all nodded.

"That's right, buddy," said Kenji, nodding so hard his mop of jet-black hair flew. "Tania's fine, you'll see."

Yusuf didn't look convinced. Come to think of it, nobody else did either. Except maybe the detective. But he didn't know Tania like we did.

* * *

Fifteen minutes later, we were outside the front entrance to the small apartment building where the Karouts and the Yates lived. After leaving X's place, there hadn't even been a discussion. It was just silently assumed that we were going to hit Tania's apartment next, in spite of what Detective Maplethorpe had told us about leaving her alone.

We needed information if we were going to figure out where Tania was. That was something else we didn't need to talk about, by the way. If the cops weren't going to look for Tania, then we would.

Yusuf's folks had become friends with Tania's mom over the winter, after Yusuf and Tania had started hanging out together. None of us except Yusuf had met her, but Yusuf told us she was divorced from a deadbeat named Johnnie Billingsley, and she had gladly changed back to her family name of Yates after the split.

But the divorce had been ugly, and most of the ugliness had been around custody of Tania. Lots of nasty letters, phone calls, and eventually threats from Johnnie to just grab his daughter sometime when Winnie wasn't looking.

Luckily the dude lived two states away, in Pennsylvania, and had no money, so he wasn't an immediate threat, but I bet you understand why a mother would be a little worried anyway. Now that Tania hadn't shown up after our gig, naturally Johnnie Billingsley was the first person Tania's mom thought of.

I looked up as we went into the building and saw a small broadcasting antenna on the roof, maybe ten feet tall and painted red and white — the ham radio antenna Tania had told me about. I was pretty impressed. It must have taken some serious work to get that thing up.

Inside, Yusuf told us that the Yates lived up on the fifth floor. There was a small elevator in the lobby and a door that led to a flight of stairs. Yusuf pushed the elevator button.

"I'll meet you guys up there," I said, going to the stairway door.

Yusuf looked puzzled. "Don't you want to take the elevator, Carlos?"

I shook my head. "No way, man. Claustrophobia. Big time. I don't do elevators. Or any other enclosed spaces. Nope."

"C-man ain't lyin'" said X. "I went camping with him and his folks once. There was this cave tour we all went on, except for—"

"Yeah, okay, X," I said. "They get it, man. See you guys on five." I went through the door and started climbing.

A few minutes later, I met my bandmates outside the Yates apartment, sweating and breathing hard. I'd run up the five flights of stairs, hoping to beat them, but no dice.

"Man, sure was hard work ridin' that elevator," said X, rubbing his leg muscles. "Carlos, how'd you know the stairs'd be easier?"

"Shut it, Xavier," I told him. "We'll see who's dead at fifty of a heart attack and who isn't."

"Come on, you two," said Kenji. "Stop screwing around and let's do this."

We clustered around the apartment door. There was a small wreath of wildflowers hung on the door, along with a hand-lettered sign that said "Home Is Where The Heart Is" in pink balloon letters on a square of laminated posterboard in a light brown wood frame.

Big hearts were drawn all around the letters in red, pink, yellow, and purple. Through the door came the sound of a TV preacher giving a loud sermon.

Yusuf knocked on the door.

The preacher's voice was abruptly cut off. A soft voice on the other side of the door said, "Yes? Who's there?" The voice had a trace of a southern twang.

"Hi, Miz Yates," said Yusuf. "It's Yusuf Karout. I'm here with three friends. May we come in and talk to you? Just for a few minutes?"

There was a long silence. Then Winnie Yates said, "If it's about Tania, I don't think I can right now, Yusuf." I heard a note of weariness in her voice.

"I know how upset you are, Miz Yates," Yusuf said. "My friends and I know that the police won't do anything yet. We want to help find her. One of the guys with me is Xavier Maplethorpe. He—"

Yusuf was cut short by the apartment door opening a little bit, enough for Winnie Yates to look out at us. She was short and thin, with a round face and round eyes behind big round glasses. The eyes were bloodshot and there were lines on her face that I was pretty sure hadn't been there twenty-four hours ago. If I had to guess, I'd say she was in her forties, but the lines added ten years.

"Xavier?" she said, looking at all of us before focusing on X's six-foot height and huge Afro. "You're Xavier Maplethorpe? Zeinab Karout told me what you did for her family. You and your friends." A smile crossed her face, instantly making her look ten years younger. "And you two must be Carlos and Kenji," she said, looking at us and nodding.

"Yes, ma'am," said Kenji. "We're awfully sorry about Tania. We want to help."

"True dat," said X. "Can we come in, Miz Yates?"

"Of course you can." She swung the door open and stood aside, ushering us in.

The apartment was small and neat. It was a copy of Yusuf's place down the hall. There were framed pictures of Tania covering the walls. One in particular caught my eye: in it, Tania was maybe eight years old, dressed in a bright white T-shirt with a print of Bob Marley's face colored in the yellow, green, and black stripes of the Jamaican flag.

She was standing in what looked like a small field or vacant lot, and behind her was some kind of clubhouse or fort made of scrap lumber and tree branches. The entrance was a rusty screen door, probably scavenged from somebody's garbage. Over the entrance was nailed a white-painted two-by-four with the words "Tania's Palace" drawn in heavy black letters on it.

On the muted TV, the preacher, a tall dude with shellacked blonde hair wearing a gray three-piece suit with a large gold cross pinned to the lapel, was continuing his sermon, his mouth opening and closing silently. His hands waved wildly around his head.

Scattered across a large glass coffee table were dozens of color copies of a flier featuring a large picture of Tania and information about her disappearance, along with a phone number in big block letters. Next to the fliers was a small, clear plastic case. The case was open. Inside were what looked like four or five syringes and a little glass vial. Tania's name was written on the outside of the case in black marker.

Kenji must have noticed it, too, because he said, "Yusuf, you never mentioned Tania being diabetic."

"I didn't know she was," said Yusuf. "She never told me anything about that."

"My daughter doesn't like people to know unless they have to," Winnie said, and gestured for us to sit down.

There was a worn but comfortable-looking sofa, and X and I sank down onto it, discovering it was even comfier than it looked. Yusuf and Kenji took seats in a couple of high-backed armchairs.

"God bless her, she's embarrassed by it for some reason. I don't understand it. I've told her that God made her that way and it's nothing to be ashamed of."

"Right on," said X, clearly impatient to get down to business. "But she'll be needing that stuff, right?"

Winnie nodded and her unhappy look deepened, making her look even older. "That's right, X. I'm very worried. Without her needles and her insulin she has no way to give herself injections. If she doesn't get her injections... she'll be..." She trailed off, and tears came to her eyes.

Yusuf took her hand. "We understand, Miz Yates." Then, to us: "You guys know what this means, right?"

"Yeah," said Kenji, frowning. "It means we're on the clock. We need to find out what happened and reunite

Tania with her supplies in, what, like three days at the most?"

X shook his head. His beachball-sized Afro floated around his head like a dark brown halo. "Less than that. Without insulin, your cells can't absorb sugar from your blood, dig? Your cells starve, which means you starve. But it ain't like not eating for a few days. That wouldn't ki—" He broke off, glancing at Tania's mom. "That wouldn't do much harm.

"Without insulin, your body starts using up its own fat real fast. When your body burns its own fat, it makes these chemicals called ketones. Ketones are most uncool, fellas. Those build up in your bloodstream and... well, you got big problems, let's put it that way. No, we have maybe twenty-four hours, best-case scenario. Miz Yates, is there anything you can tell us about the night of the gig that might help us find Tania?"

"Well, Tania was going to meet me for dinner at the Hamburger Palace afterward," she said. "I was there and waited for an hour. I called her phone several times. She never answered. She never showed up." She looked like she might start crying. "Oh, Tania, where did you go?" she said softly, almost to herself. "Where are you, baby?"

Yusuf, who was still holding her hand, gave it a squeeze. She looked at him and smiled a little. "Thanks, Yusuf. I can see why Tania likes you."

That little factoid took none of us by surprise... except Yusuf. He looked a little shell-shocked and struggled to find a reply. But Winnie rescued him from his tongue-tied state by continuing on about what happened Saturday night.

"There's a shortcut she sometimes takes if she's going to Hamburger Palace from school. She often goes there with her friends when classes let out. It's a vacant lot with a little creek running through it. She calls it her hideout. She used to play there when she was a girl. She and her little friends would make up all sorts of games and adventures. It's kind of her own little kingdom."

"Is that where that picture was taken?" I asked, pointing at the photo of young Tania standing in front of the scrap-lumber fort.

Winnie nodded. "That's it. That little fort... She and her friends built that." She sounded proud. "Took them a whole summer, but they did it. 'Tania's Palace,' that's what they called it. They built it strong, too. It's still there, in fact."

"Where is this vacant lot?" asked X. "Sounds like that should be our next stop."

8

The footprints were still fresh.

The four of us were at the edge of the big vacant lot, bending over and looking at a set of footprints that led off into the little patch of scrub forest that dominated the lot. They were big, at least a size 11, and had a waffle pattern that looked like some kind of work boot or hiking boot. The ground was soft here, and the prints were easy to see.

There was a second set of prints, much smaller, with a tennis-shoe pattern, next to the boot prints.

"Smaller ones must be Tania," I said.

"Yeah," said X. "That's what I was thinking, too. Man, whoever went after her was a big dude."

He pulled his phone out of a back pocket and started snapping pics of the prints. When he was done, we started walking deeper into the vacant lot, following the tracks as they entered the sparse forest. Sunlight slanted down through leaves overhead, making a patchwork of light and shadow on the ground. An unseasonably warm breeze made the branches rattle.

It didn't take long before we found where the footprints led: right to Tania's childhood fort. It looked nearly the same as it did in the picture in the Yates apartment, although the wood was faded and weatherbeaten now and the door was missing. But it looked solid, and I was impressed the thing was still standing after so many years.

I stared at the sign over the entrance. "Tania's Palace" was still visible on the two-by-four, but the lettering was faded, not dark and fresh-looking like I'd seen in the photo of Tania in the apartment.

"Are we gonna go in?" said Yusuf. "Or are we gonna just stand here all day?"

"Chill, bro," said X. "Lemme just check around the outside first, okay?"

Yusuf didn't look happy. I felt for the guy. As worried as we all were about Tania, I knew Yusuf's concern was ten times bigger. It was obvious to everyone that he had fallen for her. Hard.

X walked slowly around the perimeter of the fort, examining the scrap lumber closely, especially the door frame, which was made of more two-by-fours. He stopped by the left-hand door jamb. He pointed to something and we moved in for a closer look. There were holes in the wood, small ones, with bright, freshly-torn wood splinters sticking out of them. There was a cluster of three up near our heads, and another cluster down by our knees.

"The door got ripped out," said Kenji, squinting through his thick glasses at the holes.

"Right on, bassman," said X. "But check this, too." He carefully pulled something off of a splinter of wood sticking out of the doorframe at about chest height. It was a small piece of black cloth, about an inch square. He pulled out a small, high-powered magnifying glass. "The edges are all frayed. Cotton fibers, I'm pretty sure. Only one way a piece of dyed cotton gets stuck to a fort in the middle of a vacant lot."

"It came from someone's clothes," said Yusuf.

"Bingo, dude. This was a lucky find. The really good news is that cotton fibers are like magnets for all kinds of environmental debris. Dust, soil, pollen, anything that's airborne and comes in small particles is gonna cling onto cotton." He pulled a small Ziploc bag out of one pocket and deposited the piece of cloth inside. He zipped it shut and stuck it back in his pocket.

"Never know," he said. "Might find something interesting when I check it out at home."

"Okay, that's really cool and everything, X," said Yusuf, his tone telling all of us he considered X's find to be anything but cool. "Now can we go inside the fort?"

"Right on."

He stepped into the fort's dim interior, and the rest of us followed.

I immediately felt like I didn't want to be there. The interior was dim and cool, sunlight filtering through in dusty shafts through gaps in the plywood roof. The walls were also plywood, slotted into the ground deeply enough to make them stable.

The missing door lay against one wall. The wood frame was splintered and the screen was torn in several places, but I still recognized it from Winnie Yates' photo. The door's hinges, rusted strips of metal with screws dangling from them, hung at odd, twisted angles. I noticed my bandmates also staring at the door, and I know we were all thinking the same thing: someone tore that door off and tossed it there.

The fort was bigger on the inside than I thought it would be, and I realized that Tania and her friends, when they'd built it, had dug into the embankment behind the fort a couple of feet to make extra floor space. The concrete wall that should have formed the back wall of the fort was gone. I could see ragged edges of it sticking out a couple of inches behind where the scrap lumber walls met the embankment. The place looked pretty solid, and I guessed Tania had had some help from someone who knew what they were doing.

"Hey, Yusuf," I said, and my drummer jumped a little at my voice. He'd been staring at the door, too. "Is Tania's dad a carpenter? Work in construction or anything?"

He nodded. "Yeah, he does. He must have helped build this."

"Exactly what I was thinking. I can't see any eight-year-old kids making a fort this solid."

"Good call," said X. "But that means her pops knows where this place is." He didn't have to finish his thought. The footprints leading to the fort suddenly seemed more ominous.

The excavated soil of the embankment formed the fort's rear wall, and against this leaned a large piece of corrugated steel, maybe four feet square. X approached it, checking the ground carefully. The floor of the fort was packed earth that had been cleared of vegetation long ago. He was bent over almost double, his huge fro almost sweeping against the dirt. He stepped slowly forward as the rest of us watched, until his head bumped into the sheet of metal.

"Ow," he said mildly. "Good thing I got big hair, or that woulda left a welt."

None of us felt like laughing. There was a bad vibe in that place. Maybe it was just the knowledge that there was a friend of ours somewhere who could be in serious need of medical help, but there was something oppressive about the place. Like it was haunted.

I thought of the photo of little Tania standing in front of this very place, her grin as bright as the sun, and the bold, fresh lettering of the sign over the door, which was solidly attached to its frame. Looking around the place now, I could almost believe it was haunted.

It didn't help that the image of those diabetes needles and vials in the Yates apartment kept popping up in my head. It was a constant reminder that it had been over twelve hours since Tania disappeared, and she could be in really bad shape. Or worse. Looking at the faces of my friends, I knew that thought wasn't far from their minds, either.

X broke me out of my depressing train of thought. "Check this, brothers." He was pointing to the dirt in front of the corrugated steel. It looked subtly different than the rest of the floor.

As if reading my mind, X said, "This dirt's been brushed."

He was right. Instead of looking trampled like the rest of the fort's floor, it was smooth, and there were faint lines across it, all running in the same direction. Like someone had taken a broom to it.

"Why would someone—" Kenji began to say, but Yusuf cut him off.

"To hide something," he said, getting down on one knee next to X and looking closely at the ground.

"Like what?" said Kenji.

Yusuf and X looked at each other. "Like marks from something big and heavy bein' dragged across here," X said, and Yusuf nodded. "About what you were thinking, brother?"

"Yeah," said Yusuf, pointing. There was a faint groove dug into the dirt that the brushing hadn't quite erased. The groove extended about three feet and ended at one corner of the piece of corrugated metal. Just like someone had moved it over the dirt, then tried to erase the marks from it.

We stared at the big metal sheet for what felt like a long time, not saying anything. The faint hum of traffic out on Grand River drifted through the air.

Yusuf got us moving by grabbing one edge of the metal with both hands.

"What are you guys staring at?" he said. "This thing isn't going to move itself!"

X, Kenji, and I grabbed edges also, and we all pushed, trying to tip the thing away from earth embankment.

In case you didn't already know, corrugated steel is heavy. I didn't know how heavy until that day in Tania's Palace, when it took all four of us to push the sheet far enough from the embankment to make it begin to tip forward. After that, gravity did the work, and the steel square hit the ground with a thud that made my feet vibrate, and it kicked up a cloud of choking dust. After we were done coughing and sneezing, we looked at the wall of dirt that had been hidden until moments before.

In the center of it was the black, gaping mouth of a tunnel. And from the darkness inside, very faintly, we could hear tapping.

Tania's Palace

9

Remember how I'm claustrophobic?

The reason I bring it up is the fact that, as it turned out, I was the only one short and skinny enough to crawl into that tunnel.

It was an old drainage culvert, lined with cement, and it was only about a foot and a half across. Wet, mildewy smells drifted out of it like poison gas. There was no water in it, at least not here at the end of it. Who knew what there might be further in?

Yusuf, of course, was the first one to volunteer to crawl in. In fact, he practically dove into the culvert as soon as we tipped over the steel plate. But, even though the dude is short, he's not exactly thin: he's got some pretty serious muscle on him. He got in as far as his shoulders, then backed out again, looking angry and scared.

"Someone's in there," he said as he brushed dead leaves and dirt out of his hair. "That tapping. Someone's making that noise."

He was right, and we all knew it. The pattern the taps made wasn't random, and it wasn't just a steady, monotonous noise, either, like you'd expect if it had been dripping water. The taps came in clusters, and they stopped and started at intervals that weren't even, but definitely weren't random, either. I began to recognize the patterns from old spy movies I'd seen.

"That sounds like Morse code!" I said.

Kenji and Yusuf looked at me with surprise, but X nodded. "Sure is, C-man." He looked grim. "I don't like what it's sayin', either."

Yusuf turned three shades paler. "What's that?" he asked. "What does it say?"

X spoke slowly, listening to the taps as he did so, as if to confirm the message. "It says 'Help... help... help.' That's it."

"Oh, God," said Yusuf, and began murmuring fast in Arabic. I think he was praying. I think maybe we all were, in one way or another.

"Carlos," said X, looking at me. "You gotta go in there, my brother. Yusuf won't fit. I won't, either, 'cause I'm too tall. I might not be able to maneuver around even if I did get in. Kenji's out, too. He's got too much around the waistline."

"Sorry," said Kenji, looking at me. "He's right, Carlos. That leaves you."

He and X and Yusuf looked at me.

"Sorry, brother," said X. "I know you hate the tight spaces and all, but..."

"Forget it," I said, trying to sound brave and feeling about as far from it as you can get. "If I gotta go, then I'm going. Gimme your flashlight, X."

X fished in his backpack, produced the mini Maglight he kept in it, and handed it over to me. I turned it on to make sure it was working. A bright beam of light stabbed the darkness at the culvert's entrance, showing fuzzy green moss growing on the tunnel's concrete floor.

The tapping continued as I took a deep breath and tried to prepare myself.

"That's it, just breathe, man, just relax," said X. "You got this."

"Right," said Yusuf. "No problem, Carlos. You'll kick that tunnel's butt."

Kenji just nodded and gave me two thumbs up.

I got down on my hands and knees at the entrance to the culvert. The dank odor was even stronger, and the flashlight beam penetrated maybe twenty feet in before being swallowed up by the shadows deeper inside. A fresh breeze passed over my face, which felt clammy and cool. I realized I was sweating.

Calm down, man, I told myself, and took more long breaths.

Brittle, dead leaves crunched under my hands and knees as I crawled forward and stuck my head and shoulders inside. I had maybe two inches of clearance on either side of my shoulders. I kept the flashlight gripped tightly in my right hand, the beam aimed ahead of me. A few more inches in, then a foot, then two feet. Then I felt the toes of my sneakers dragging against concrete instead of dirt and I knew I was all the way in.

The tapping kept up its monotonous Morse code pattern, but I was pretty sure it was starting to get fainter instead of louder as I inched my way further in. I knew that couldn't be a good thing.

"Don't think, don't think, don't think," I started saying to myself softly. My voice sounded flat and dead inside the concrete passageway. "Don't think, don't think, don't think."

"Go, man, go!" I heard X yell from behind me. "You're doin' righteously good!"

X's voice sounded like it was coming from the moon, even though I knew my friends, and sunlight and fresh air, couldn't be any more than two feet behind me.

I pushed forward, willing my arms and legs to work when every cell in my body was telling me to back up, back up, back up, get out of here, get out...

Another couple of feet forward. The bottom of the culvert was covered in old moss, making a soft carpet. *At least I don't have to scrape myself up on bare cement,* I thought. *Although some battle scars would look kinda cool.*

I kept going, a few more feet in, then a few more. Ahead, the pipe narrowed into blackness. I kept going, shuffling over the moss-covered concrete, smelling dank air and dead vegetation. A little further, a little further.

After about ten minutes, I figured I must be at least a hundred feet down the tunnel, and I began to think this might actually be okay.

Then the first wave of true panic washed over me.

Imagine the worst thing you've ever felt, times ten. That's what this felt like. My heart began hammering against my ribcage and my breath started coming in short gasps. Against my will, the image of being stuck inside a narrow stone throat rose in my mind. I moaned and tried to shove it back down into my subconscious, but now that it was there, it stayed.

Me, a little Mexican-American morsel, wedged in some stone giant's concrete esophagus, nothing but blackness and death ahead. My chest felt constricted, like it was caught in an invisible, giant fist. The flashlight beam jittered wildly as my hands shook. Sweat dripped in my eyes, making them sting.

I bit down on a scream, clamping my jaws together and hearing my teeth grind against each other. I knew if I screamed it was all over. If I let myself scream, I'd either wriggle my way back out of the culvert and never go back in again, Tania or no Tania, or I'd just pass out from sheer fright. I couldn't allow that to happen.

With my eyes squeezed shut, feeling the cool, dank air around me and smelling the odor of old mildew and rotting leaves, I gradually began to get myself back under control. Bit by agonizing bit, the sense of being squeezed in a stone throat receded, and my heart rate began to slow to something close to normal. I forced myself to take long, deep breaths, in through my nose and out through my mouth. Slowly, slowly, I opened my eyes again.

Everything was black. The flashlight had gone out.

Tania's Palace

10

This time, I think I actually did pass out. At least for a second. And the only reason I didn't collapse is because I was jammed into a three-foot-wide concrete pipe.

When I'd fought the panic down to a level that allowed some rational thought, I realized it wasn't completely black in the culvert. A little bit of light filtered down from the entrance. I heard my friends back there, calling to me, but my head was swimming too much to understand what they were saying.

Breathe, I told myself.

I breathed. Then I flicked the flashlight on and off several times. Nothing happened.

I still had the flashlight in my right hand. With my left, I found the end cap on the back of the metal tube, the part that unscrews to allow access to the batteries. Feeling it with one fingertip, I noticed a gap. Somehow the cap had come partly unscrewed. With a quick prayer to the gods of light, I tightened the cap back into place.

Nothing.

I nearly screamed in frustration before I remembered the on-off switch. I clicked it with my right thumb.

Sweet, blessed light filled the tunnel ahead of me. I never imagined how glad I'd be to see the mossy, cracked cement again. It felt like I'd been in the dark for an hour, although I knew it couldn't have been more than a couple of minutes.

"I'm okay!" I yelled, not knowing if my bandmates could hear me or not. It didn't matter. I said it more for myself than anyone else.

It was then that I noticed the tapping had stopped.

At some point while the flashlight had been out, it had stopped, and in my panic I hadn't noticed.

"Hey!" I yelled. "Hey, Tania, is that you?" My words died a few feet ahead of me in the culvert's stagnant air. "Tania Yates! That you?"

At first, nothing. Then, very faintly, a few more taps. Then silence again.

Get your butt moving, Villareal!

I got my butt moving, shuffling forward again, the flashlight's bright beam lighting the way. I had to be at least fifteen feet into the embankment by now, I figured, but it was hard to judge distance. I tried not to think about the thousands of pounds of dirt right over my head.

Keep moving. Keep moving.

A few more weak taps, but they sounded much closer now.

Keep moving.

Cold cement brushed against my shoulders. To take my mind off where I was, I thought about Tania's dad, Johnnie Billingsley. Those footprints through the vacant lot were too big to be anything but those of a large man, and like Yusuf had told us, old Johnnie was huge. If it turned out he'd chased Tania into this hellhole and then left her here, I would personally kick him in the crotch so hard he'd be singing falsetto the rest of his life. And that was just for starters.

I stopped and listened, trying to control my panting, which echoed down the tunnel. I didn't hear any tapping.

Further. A few more feet. Green moss under my hands and knees, curved concrete all around, dank smell of old vegetation filling my nose. I hated this place already. A few more feet.

Then, suddenly, there she was.

11

She was lying slumped against the right side of the tunnel, just at the edge of the flashlight beam. Beyond her, the tunnel was shrouded in darkness. Her head was lying sideways against one shoulder, her long, dark cornrows hanging in her face. In one hand she held a chunk of concrete that she must have been using to bang against the wall of the culvert. She wasn't moving now, though.

"Tania!" I said, covering the distance between us as fast as the cramped space would let me. I turned my head as if to look back over my shoulder. "Hey, guys, I found Tania!" I shouted, having no idea if they could hear me. "Get some help here, quick!"

I could tell she was breathing, and I put my index and middle fingers against her neck, searching for her pulse. It was weak, but it was there. I gently pushed her cornrows aside to reveal her face.

Her eyes were closed, her mouth slightly open, her breath moving in and out in faint whispers. Her skin, normally a dark mocha, looked several shades paler. She was wearing the same clothes she'd worn to our gig the night before, but they were filthy and torn in several places. On her left foot was a mud-spattered white Ked. The other shoe wasn't anywhere in sight, and we hadn't seen it in or around the fort.

"Tania?" I said, close to her ear. "Tania? You there? Can you hear me?"

She moaned once, softly.

"I'm gonna get you out of here," I said.

The culvert was too narrow for me to turn around. I would have to drag her out backwards. Putting the flashlight in my mouth so it shone straight ahead, I carefully leaned Tania over until she was lying flat on the tunnel floor with her feet, one sneakered and the other bare, facing me. I gripped her ankles firmly, and began to back up, pulling as I went.

She was heavy.

Until that moment, I'd had no idea how heavy people really are. Especially when you're dragging them along rough concrete while crawling. Backwards. I had to move in a stop-and-go fashion, shuffling backward a foot or so, then pulling Tania toward me, then doing it again.

It was hard work, and every few feet Tania would moan again. The noise echoed eerily down the tunnel, raising the hairs on the back of my neck and threatening to bring back my claustrophobic panic. I fought it off and kept going: shuffle back, pull, shuffle back, pull. Don't think.

A stone throat. And you're stuck inside it.

"Shut up," I said around the flashlight, making the beam wobble and cast weird shadows on the curved walls of the culvert. "Just shut it."

Another shuffle. Another pull. Shuffle, pull. Shuffle, pull.

That's when the flashlight went out.

Well, technically it didn't just go out. See, I dropped it first. It fell out of my teeth. It hit the floor of the culvert and BANG. I heard a tiny sound of breaking glass and knew the bulb had shattered.

I was in total darkness.

Stone throat. Stuck in this narrow, constricted stone throat. Trapped.

"Shut. Up." I growled this through clenched teeth as I tried to fight down a wave of black terror. My elbows brushed against either side of the pipe, the pipe that was just barely wide enough for me, the pipe I had to back up for who knew how far before I could get out into the fresh air and blue sky.

And that's what did it.

The image of blue sky, and the knowledge that I was buried in this cement tunnel deep inside a hill far away from that sky, sent me over the edge into full-blown, howling panic.

84

12

At some point during my meltdown I must have passed out, because when I came back to my senses I was lying in my own bed, in my own house, and there was a splint on the little finger of my right hand.

The bedroom window was open, and through it I could see blue sky with a few cumulus clouds drifting by. A cool breeze drifted through the room. I closed my eyes and breathed deeply, praying this wasn't just a hallucination and that I wasn't still down in that pipe.

I opened my eyes again, saw the sky through the window again, felt the softness of my pillow under my head, and smelled the scent of the lilac bush that grew in our backyard coming in on the breeze. I knew it was all real.

"Yeah, baby!" I yelled to the bedroom. "No tunnel's gonna beat me, man!"

"Carlos?" It was my mom's voice, outside my room. The door cracked open, and she peeked in. "Carlos, you're finally awake! My baby's awake!" She turned her head to call down the hallway. "Everyone? Carlos is awake! He's awake!"

Everyone?

It became clear a moment later who she meant by "everyone." A regular mob crowded through the door and stood around my bed, everybody grinning.

My dad was there. Both he and my mom had been worrying a lot, I could tell, and I felt bad. But only for a second, because my bandmates, Tania, and Tania's mom were there, too.

Winnie Yates didn't say anything at first, but she bent down and planted a big kiss on my cheek.

Then she took my uninjured hand and squeezed it. She looked like she might cry.

"Thank you, Carlos, thank you so very much for what you did, pulling my girl out of that place. I can't express how grateful I am to you and your three friends here."

"It's all good, Miz Yates," I said. My throat felt raw for some reason. I realized I must have done a lot of screaming inside that culvert. I wondered if anyone had heard it.

"Dude!" said X. "When we heard you screamin' your head off in there, we all thought that was it, baby! Like, we thought you'd gone cuckoo on us!"

That answered that question.

"Yeah," said Kenji. "We'd already called the cops when we heard you say you found Tania. But they weren't there yet, and none of us could get in to find out what was wrong. All we could do was stand there in that fort, listening to you hollering."

Yusuf spoke up. On his head was his trademark straw cowboy hat with the American flag bandanna tied around it. I saw the hole in one side where Derek Bodley had torn out some of the straw the previous summer. Yusuf had never gotten it fixed. I think it was a badge of pride for him.

"Thank you, Carlos, for what you did for Tania. You're a true friend."

"Yeah, Carlos, thank you," said Tania.

She was standing next to Yusuf and, I noticed, without much surprise, that they were holding hands. She still looked a little tired but otherwise in good shape considering what she'd been through.

"That sounds so lame compared to what you did. How about this?" She let go of Yusuf's hand and came close to me. She bent down and planted a kiss on my cheek, the opposite one her mom had smooched. Now I'd been anointed by two generations of Yates women.

"When those guys were chasing me, I didn't know where to go, but if I'd known what was going to happen I never would've gone in that pipe," Tania said.

"Yeah, about that," I said, sitting up a bit. "Who *did* chase you in there? How'd it all go down?" I looked down at the splint on my hand. "And what'd I do to my finger?"

X laughed, making his giant Afro bob and weave. Seeing that, and Yusuf's hat, and the loud Hawaiian shirt Kenji was wearing, it hit me how much these guys meant to me, and how being in that hole, even for a little while, made me appreciate life more.

"My brothers and sisters," he said to everyone there, "get comfy, 'cause this is gonna take some time."

13

"After Tania left the gig," said X, "she was going to meet her mom at the Burger Palace, remember? And we were right, she decided to take a shortcut through that vacant lot. When she was about halfway across the lot" — he glanced at Tania, who nodded — "two dudes came out of nowhere and started chasing her."

"Who?" I asked. "Who was it? It was Tania's dad, wasn't it? Billingsley?"

"Nope," said X, and I got my first of what would be several surprises. "But I'll get to that in a bit, you dig? Anyway, these two knuckleheads were wearing ski masks, so Tania didn't know who they were. They didn't say anything, either. Well, Tania panicked. Freaked out. Like, who wouldn't right? Two masked fellas coming out of the shadows and coming after you when you're by yourself.

"Anyway, she ran for her old fort, remembering the entrance to the culvert inside it. Turns out, she used to go in there when she was a little squirt, her and her friends, and pretend they were rescuing prisoners from an evil king's dungeon." He pointed at Tania. "Gotta give you props on the imagination there. Very cool."

"Somebody had to save those people," said Tania, and everyone laughed. "Never thought I'd need saving from there, though."

"So who was it, if it wasn't her dad?" I asked.

X looked at me. "Three guesses, first two don't count."

It dawned on me what he meant. "You're not saying... No, no way. Uh-uh."

But X nodded. "Yeah, man. It was him. Our old buddy Derek Bodley."

"But he's a little guy," I objected. "No way he made those big prints."

"He didn't. Remember, there were two dudes. The other one made the prints. The other one has big feet. Derek probably just made sure to step in the bigger prints so he wouldn't leave any of his own."

"So who—"

"His dad," said X, anticipating my question. "Mister Vincent Bodley. He was the other chaser. It was a father-son operation."

"Wait," I said, shifting in the bed and throwing off a blanket. It was getting warm in the room. Seven people put out a lot of body heat. "How do you know all this, X? How do you know it was Derek and his dad?"

"I took photos of the footprints, remember? Then, yesterday, me and my man Kenji snuck over to the Bodley place and found some muddy footprints leading from the yard into the house. I snapped pics of those and guess what? Perfect match. Same size, even the same tread pattern."

"So maybe whoever went after Tania has the same boots as Vince Bodley," I said.

"Maybe," said X. "But remember that little scrap of cloth I grabbed from outside the fort?"

"Yeah."

"I took a peek at it with my scope. Know what I found?" X was grinning, showing his perfect, white teeth. He could hardly contain himself. "Pollen, brothers and sisters. Pollen. You dig me?" He cut a little James Brown move right there in my bedroom.

"So?" said Kenji. "I bet all of us have some pollen sticking to our clothes right now. It's spring time. The air's full of the stuff."

"Sure," said X. "Pollen from local trees and whatnot. But I bet none of us has pollen from *avicennia germinans*." The way he said it, you could hear the italics.

"Avi-what?" I said.

"The black mangrove tree. Its scientific name is *avicennia germinans*."

"Black mangrove?" I said, remembering where I'd heard those words recently. "Didn't Bodley tell us last Thursday that his dad sent him to live with his uncle in Florida? The uncle who lived—"

"In a black mangrove swamp. Yep. And he just got back. Spent the winter there. Guess whatever shirt he wore when he and his pops were chasing Tania, he also wore down in Florida."

"And didn't wash," observed Kenji.

"X, what can I say?" said Yusuf. "You are the man!"

They exchanged high-fives, X having to bend down a bit from his six-foot altitude to match Yusuf's five-foot-four.

Tania's Palace

14

"Hang on a sec," I said, realizing something. "If you did all this after me and Tania got out of the tunnel, how long have I been out? And by the way, how did we get out of there?"

My mom spoke up. "You've been sleeping for" — she checked her watch — "almost fifty-two hours, Carlos."

I couldn't believe it. "Two days? I've been out for two whole days?"

"And then some," added Kenji, unhelpfully.

"Oh man, call me Rip Van Winkle," I said.

"Yeah, or maybe Sleeping Beauty," said X. "Anyway, the cops we called finally got to the fort, and luckily one of them was a smaller guy. Officer Dale Jones. He's the one who dragged you out of that pipe. Then he went back in and dragged Tania out, too."

"Thank you Officer Jones," I said. "Wherever you are."

"Oh, don't worry," said X. "My pops is already working on getting you a chance to meet him and say thanks in person."

"Cool," I said. "Hey, Tania, how're you feeling? It was diabetic shock or something, wasn't it? That's why you passed out when I found you. And, by the way, big props on the Morse code! I guess you couldn't yell."

Tania shook her head. "I couldn't talk at all by the time you found me. I didn't even remember who you were. I heard you guys talking out in the fort, but I was too weak to call out. So I tapped with that piece of concrete.

"And yeah, it was super-high blood sugar from not being able to take my insulin. That's why I was so sick. Another few hours and..." Tania shook her head again, unwilling to say what I knew we were all thinking. "Anyway, I owe you big time, Carlos. And all of you guys." She took Yusuf's hand and squeezed it.

"Not a chance," I said. "You don't owe us anything. You just take good care of our drummer, okay? He's a genius on the skins, and geniuses need lots of TLC."

Yusuf looked happy and embarrassed at the same time. "Don't listen to him, Tania, okay? He crawled down a pipe and then spent two days sound asleep. He doesn't know what he's saying."

"I think he's exactly right, mister," said Tania, and kissed him full on the lips.

"Man, get a room, you two!" said X in mock horror. "No PDA while I'm expounding, please! Now, where was I?"

"The cop pulled me out of the culvert," I said.

"Right. So after you and Tania were out, they took both of you to the hospital to get checked out. Tania recovered pretty fast, once they got some insulin in her. They didn't find anything wrong with you, C-man. They figured you just got exhausted from crawling in there and trying to pull her out."

And from panicking once or twice, I thought, but didn't say.

"So what now?" I asked.

"What now?" said X. "The 'what now' is already over, bro. I brought everything we found to my pops, who passed it on to one of his friends in the Redford P.D. Bodleys got a visit from them just this morning. My pops got the whole 411 on what went down. At first Derek and his dad tried to deny everything, of course. But they're lousy liars. They got taken in for questioning, and they ended up making a full confession."

"They admitted it?" I said in disbelief.

X nodded. "Sure did. Neither of those dudes has any backbone when they're up against the wall like that."

"So, X," said Tania, "why'd they do this in the first place? Derek only met me once and his dad doesn't know me at all. You think maybe it's because I'm black?"

"I know why they did it," said Yusuf. "Because of me."

"Because of you?" Tania repeated. "Oh, wait, that whole thing last summer..."

Yusuf nodded. "Yeah. Derek Bodley hates me worse than anything, ever since he got caught trying to frame me and have my family deported. And he knew that you and I are... you know..."

"Dude, go ahead and say it, man!" I said. "You two are an item. Boyfriend-girlfriend, sweethearts, going steady, whatever you wanna call it. It's obvious to everyone, am I right?"

Everyone in the room smiled and nodded agreement.

"Plain as Jane," said X. "Property of Captain Obvious. Clear as the purest crystal—"

"Shut up, X!" said Yusuf, but he was smiling, too. "Okay, yeah, he did it because he knows Tania's my girlfriend and he wanted to get revenge for last summer." He looked at Tania. "Sorry."

"You've got nothing to be sorry about, Yusuf," interjected Tania's mom. "That whole Bodley clan is rotten to the core. I could tell you some stories from when I was a little girl in this neighborhood, and Vince Bodley was the local bully. Been going on seems like forever. You probably saved Tania's life, young man."

"That's what the doctors told me," said Tania. "Baby, you and your friends got me out of some big trouble." She looked at X. "How'd they know where I'd be?"

I knew the answer to that one.

"Your phone," I said before X could open his mouth. He nodded agreement instead. "When he stole it from my garage last week. You had the dinner date with your mom on your phone calendar, I bet."

Tania nodded. "Yeah. But it's password protected. He doesn't seem like the hacker type."

"Nope," said X. "He's dumber than a bag of rocks. My guess is, he stole it without really thinking about it. Just took the opportunity. When he realized he might be able to find something on it to use against you and Yusuf, he found someone who knew how to hack into it. Maybe a friend from school, or maybe he paid someone. But he got into it one way or another, and found your calendar."

X frowned thoughtfully. "Did you have any notes or anything in there that would've told him you'd be cutting through the vacant lot?"

Tania shook her head. "No, nothing like that. Just the place and time."

"Yeah, that's what I figured." X frowned. "Gotta admit, peeps, that part has me kinda mystified. How'd he know where to go to find you on your way to the restaurant?"

That's when I remembered.

Tania's Palace

15

"He didn't know where Tania would be," I said. "He was at the gig. I saw him, just for a second, way in the back. I wasn't sure at the time, but it must have been him. Must've waited outside and followed her. His dad, too."

X nodded. "Yeah, makes sense."

Tania shuddered. "Makes my skin crawl thinking about it."

"So," I said. "Bodley takes Tania's phone, hacks into it somehow, sees her dinner date with her mom after our gig, waits outside the gym for her, and he and his dad follow her to the vacant lot. Then they try to grab her, and she runs for the fort because she remembers the old culvert. She crawls in, Bodley and Son don't go in after her, but instead put the piece of steel in front of the entrance."

I looked at my bandmates. "All because they wanted to get back at us for last summer." I shook my head. "Man, if Derek would put half as much brainpower into doing good stuff as he does into making trouble, he'd be elected mayor or something."

"His Honor, Mayor Derek Bodley," said Kenji thoughtfully. "Yeah, I can see that."

There was a moment of complete silence. Then everyone laughed.

"Not hardly, people," said X. "Mayor Bodley. That's a trip, for sure. For real, though, I just got some info from my pops on what's probably gonna happen next."

"They're getting tied to a giant anthill and doused with honey?" I asked, thinking of an old Western I'd seen once. A guy can always hope.

"Naw, man," said X. "Bodley Senior's been arrested for endangerment of a minor. He might actually do some jail time. And Junior's in custody, too. The cops know about the trouble he causes around here. Pops says he's probably going to juvie."

He meant juvenile detention, or jail for kids. It was one of those things everyone talked about but nobody actually knew anything about. At least, my friends and I didn't. But it looked like Derek Bodley might be learning more than he ever wanted to know.

"So he might be out of our faces?" said Tania. "Good!"

Next to her, Winnie Yates nodded agreement.

There was a knock at the bedroom door. A girl's voice came through from the hallway.

"Hey, can I come in, or what? You going to keep me out in the cold, Tania Yates? I know you're in there!"

Tania beamed. "I almost forgot! I told my cousin about what happened." She gave me a sly look. "She wants to meet the big hero that rescued me."

"Wait, what?" I said, half-rising from the bed.

But Tania already had the door open. In walked the most beautiful girl I'd ever seen in my life. You know those movies where two people meet and time kind of just slows way down and everything gets a little foggy around the edges? Stupid, right? Well, I'm here to tell you that it can actually happen.

Tania's cousin was a shorter and curvier version of Tania, with the same dark mocha skin and curly dark brown hair. When she came into the room, it was more like she swept in, like a movie star, drawing all the attention to her. She was a bundle of energy, laughing and smiling and hugging Tania and Yusuf and greeting everyone else.

Then she came over to me. I was still halfway in and halfway out of the bed, tangled in the sheets, my boxer shorts showing and my skin embarrassingly pale from the long winter we'd recently come out of.

"You're Carlos?" she asked, sounding businesslike. "You must be Carlos, I've met everyone else. And you're the only one here who's lying in bed like a lazy bum! What, did you pull off some kind of daring rescue or something? That what's got you so tired out, Carlos?"

I was speechless. I stared at her. I'm pretty sure my jaw was hanging open. I don't remember for sure.

"Well," she said after a pause of approximately two seconds. "If you're not going to introduce yourself then I'll tell you who I am. I'm Rebecca Louise Armstrong, but everyone, and I mean *everyone*, calls me Beck. Not Becky, not Becca. Just Beck. Like that German beer. Easy-peasy, right? Even a silent guy like you can handle that, right Carlos?"

Now, let me make something clear here. It might sound like this girl was kind of nasty and sarcastic. For a moment, that's exactly what I thought as I half-sat, half-stood, frozen in place, watching and listening to this human whirlwind. But I caught a spark of something in her eyes as she was talking. It was a playful kind of twinkle — that's the best way I can describe it. Like she was letting me in on a secret, and the secret was that I shouldn't take anything she was saying too seriously.

Later, after I'd gotten to know Beck really well, I would come to think of this as her "un-wink." She didn't actually wink at you, but you felt like she was when she was talking a mile a minute and you didn't know which part was truth and which part was sarcasm and she'd look at you with her un-wink, and then you'd know you were in on the joke. I liked that about her, right from that first day.

Now, as I saw her un-winking at me, I began to smile. It was a slow, helpless, slightly embarrassed smile. She saw it and sat right down on the bed next to me without waiting for an invitation. I would come to learn that this was also classic Beck: coming right in and sitting right down, and somehow making you feel like it was what you'd wanted her to do all along.

What happened next, though, put the final touch on what had gone down over the last few days, days which had been full of shocks, surprises, and twists. This was the perfect ending.

Beck Armstrong looked me square in the face and said, "Thanks for saving my cousin. You're really cute, by the way. Got a girlfriend?"

I shook my head. My mouth had gone dry.

"Good." Beck slipped her hands around the back of my head, and pulled me in for a long, deep kiss.

Yeah. That's just how she rolled, man.

About The Author

Brian Kirchner is 46 years old and teaches Geology at Henry Ford College, near Detroit, Michigan. He lives in Royal Oak, Michigan, with his wife and three kids. Brian has loved writing fiction since a very young age but took a (very) long hiatus from it while earning a doctorate in Geology and starting a family. Since taking up writing again in 2016, Brian has published a short story in the online literary magazine "Inklette," he was awarded 9th place in a Writer's Digest international poetry competition, and he has published a short humor piece at the online site "Funny in Five Hundred." Brian has also written a novel and is currently shopping it around to literary agencies.

Besides writing and teaching about rocks, Brian enjoys playing guitar and banjo, reading (just about anything), road trips, astronomy, and pizza.

About The Publisher

Story Shares is a nonprofit focused on supporting the millions of teens and adults who struggle with reading by creating a new shelf in the library specifically for them. The ever-growing collection features content that is compelling and culturally relevant for teens and adults, yet still readable at a range of lower reading levels.

Story Shares generates content by engaging deeply with writers, bringing together a community to create this new kind of book. With more intriguing and approachable stories to choose from, the teens and adults who have fallen behind are improving their skills and beginning to discover the joy of reading. For more information, visit storyshares.org.

Easy to Read. Hard to Put Down.

Made in the USA
Middletown, DE
20 January 2023